The Pop Pop Man

By: Paul Doerner

Illustrated by: Patty J. Coleman

Special thanks to:

William
Kiki & Woody
Henry
Arden

For Steve

Order this book online at www.trafford.com
or email orders@trafford.com

Most Trafford titles are also available at major online book retailers.

Print information available on the last page.

ISBN: 978-1-4251-8638-8

*Our mission is to efficiently provide the world's finest, most comprehensive book publishing
service, enabling every author to experience success. To find out how to publish your book, your
way, and have it available worldwide, visit us online at www.trafford.com*

Trafford rev. 3/19/2019

 www.trafford.com

North America & international
toll-free: 1 888 232 4444 (USA & Canada)
fax: 812 355 4082

This is Deevie. His real name is Steve, but his friends call him Deevie because they are only three years old and have trouble pronouncing the letter S.

Deevie lives in an older neighborhood near some great big office buildings where his parents work. When his mom and dad go to work, Deevie has a nanny to take care of him. Her name is Edna.

Edna comes to work every day in a big taxi cab. Edna takes care of Deevie all day long and they have lots of fun together.

When Edna arrives at the house, Deevie says goodbye to his mom and dad. He is ready for a fun day at the park with Edna.

Deevie really likes it when Edna pushes him in his stroller to the big park across from his home.

In the park, Deevie and Edna sit on a bench and blow bubbles.

Deevie loves to play on the tree swing in the park. Edna pushes him high!

Deevie hears a familiar sound,
POP Pop Pop Po p
It's the Pop Pop Man!

The Pop Pop man has a big mustache and wears a big straw hat. He rides a big tractor and cuts grass in the park. Deevie calls him the Pop Pop man because his tractor makes a sound that goes

Pop Pop Pop Pop.

One day the Pop Pop man stopped his tractor and asked Edna if Deevie could come over and sit on the tractor. Edna brought Deevie to sit on the Pop Pop man's lap to ride the tractor.

The Pop Pop man bounced Deevie up and down on his knee just like the tractor was really going. Deevie started shouting, "Pop Pop Pop Pop " making the same noise the tractor makes.

After a fun day in the park, Edna gives Deevie some cookies and milk. Edna enjoys Deevie's company as much as he enjoys his snack.

Edna gets Deevie's bed ready for his nap.
Deevie loves to snuggle in his bed for a nap.

At nap time, Deevie falls fast asleep and dreams of one day sitting on the Pop Pop man's tractor again.

Printed in the United States
By Bookmasters